MAGIC VS. BIRD
IN THE NCAA FINAL

by P.K. Daniel

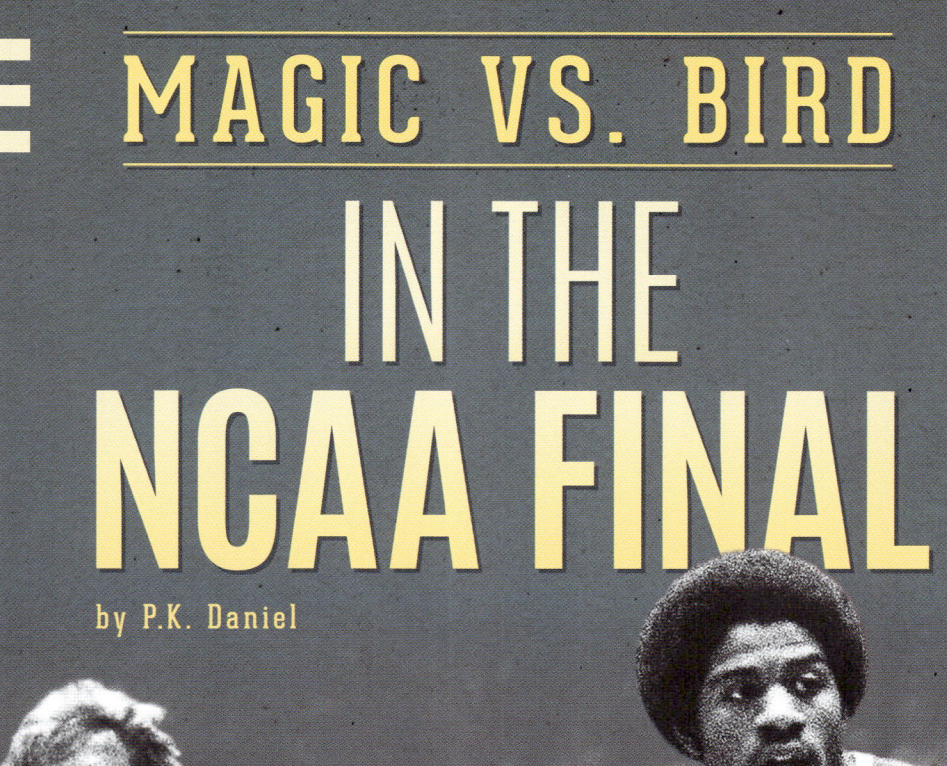

Greatest Events in SPORTS HISTORY

SportsZone
An Imprint of Abdo Publishing
www.abdopublishing.com

www.abdopublishing.com

Published by Abdo Publishing, a division of ABDO, PO Box 398166, Minneapolis, Minnesota 55439. Copyright © 2015 by Abdo Consulting Group, Inc. International copyrights reserved in all countries. No part of this book may be reproduced in any form without written permission from the publisher. SportsZone™ is a trademark and logo of Abdo Publishing.

Printed in the United States of America, North Mankato, Minnesota
102014
012015

THIS BOOK CONTAINS RECYCLED MATERIALS

Cover Photos: Brian Horton/AP Images, left; AP Images, right
Interior Photos: Brian Horton/AP Images, 1 (left); AP Images, 1 (right), 7, 14, 17, 19, 20, 25, 26, 31, 32, 35, 37; Bettmann/Corbis, 4, 23; Lennox McLendon/AP Images, 8; Charles E. Knoblock/AP Images, 11; Jack Smith/AP Images, 13; Jose R. Lopez/AP Images, 28; David J. Phillip/AP Images, 38; Amy Sancetta/AP Images, 43

Editor: Chrös McDougall
Series Designer: Craig Hinton

Library of Congress Control Number: 2014944208

Cataloging-in-Publication Data
Daniel, P.K.
 Magic vs Bird in the NCAA Final / P.K. Daniel.
  p. cm. -- (Greatest events in sports history)
ISBN 978-1-62403-596-8 (lib. bdg.)
Includes bibliographical references and index.
 1. Basketball--United States--History--Juvenile literature. 2. Basketball players--United States--Juvenile literature. 3. NCAA Basketball Tournament--History--Juvenile literature. I. Title.
 796.323--dc23
                                                                2014944208

CONTENTS

ONE
Before the Madness • 5

TWO
Practice Makes Perfect • 9

THREE
Heading to College • 15

FOUR
Building the Excitement • 21

FIVE
Game Time • 29

SIX
Legacy • 39

Timeline	44
Glossary	45
For More Information	46
Index	48
About the Author	48

Stanford University and Long Island University play a college basketball game in 1935. College basketball had no championship tournament until 1939.

CHAPTER 1

Before the Madness

It was forty years before Larry Bird and Earvin "Magic" Johnson met for the college basketball national championship. March Madness didn't yet exist. College basketball fans weren't filling out tournament brackets. Office pools weren't commonplace. ESPN wasn't that familiar friend in America's living rooms.

The year was 1939. Eight college basketball teams were invited to Northwestern University. The school's central location near Chicago made it easier for teams to attend. In Illinois, they would play in the first National Collegiate Athletic Association (NCAA) men's basketball tournament.

Basketball had been around since 1891. However, there was no official college national championship until then. The iconic

IN THE News

The *Oregon Daily Emerald* independent student newspaper ran a banner headline after the University of Oregon won the first NCAA basketball championship.

> Nation hails Ducks after 46–33 victory. They're national champions now, these tall Oregon boys who have no peer, no match wherever basketball is played in this old world. They've walked a long time and marched a long way along the nation's long trails, and now they've reached the top, the highest pinnacle for which [anyone] can strive.

Source: "Oregon National Champs." *Oregon Daily Emerald, March 28, 1939.* Print. 1.

tournament was single-elimination from the start. Little else from that tournament looked like the modern March Madness, though. The eight-team field was limited to conference champions. And the Final Four was not yet held in a football stadium. Instead, the entire tournament was played at 9,000-seat Patten Gymnasium.

The University of Oregon and Ohio State University played in the first championship game. The game was held on March 27, 1939. Official figures show that only 5,500 people showed up. Those not at the game could follow it on the radio. But the game was not

The University of California, Los Angeles, and the University of Houston play in the 1968 Final Four.

broadcast on TV. A makeshift band played "Mighty Oregon" as the Webfoots won the first NCAA title 46–33.

The game was hardly a major event. In fact, some fans and teams preferred the National Invitation Tournament (NIT). The NIT crowned its first champion in 1938 in New York City. It was not until the 1950s that the NCAA Tournament began to take over. Modern touches of March Madness were added to the tournament over the years. The tournament expanded to add more teams. Yet even into the mid-1970s, the tournament had not grown larger than 25 teams. By the end of that decade, however, no one would look at the NCAA Tournament as a niche event again.

Earvin Johnson, *left*, and Larry Bird, *right*, grew up dreaming of being star basketball players.

PRACTICE MAKES PERFECT

Larry Joe Bird was born on December 7, 1956. Earvin "Magic" Johnson was born three years later, on August 14, 1959. Both grew up in blue-collar Midwest towns. Both were great basketball players. Both learned about the game from their fathers. But that was about all they had in common. And neither set out to change college basketball.

Growing up, Johnson and Bird were kids doing what kids do. They were pretending to light the sports world on fire. Johnson would play hoops in the schoolyard in Lansing, Michigan. He'd pretend to be a National Basketball Association (NBA) star. His favorites were the Philadelphia 76ers' Wilt Chamberlain and the Detroit Pistons' Dave Bing. Johnson

IN THE News

The townspeople embraced Bird's Springs Valley basketball team. The local newspaper wrote of that support during the playoffs in Bird's senior year.

> The Springs Valley Black Hawks soared high and mighty to their 1974 Sectional Crown at Paoli by dominating Milltown, 63–46 in the championship game. The tension was mounting at least 30 minutes before the tip-off as the Valley and Milltown yell sections started [whooping] it up. You could feel the tension rising as the tip-off started when the Valley and Milltown fans seemed to rise as one unit and continued to stand throughout the game. Valley took a 16 to 12 lead at the first quarter stop, as John Carnes scored eight points and Larry Bird six.

Source: Arnold Bledsoe. "Hawks Fly to Sectional Crown." Springs Valley Herald, March 7, 1974. Print. n.p.

would even act out the part of the play-by-play announcer. But he never actually thought about becoming an NBA player for real.

Bird discovered basketball at age 13. He would shoot buckets on a hoop mounted to the garage next to his small home in French Lick, Indiana. It quickly became obvious that Bird was really good.

Bird grew to love basketball, too. But the sport also served as an escape. Life could be hard growing up in the hardscrabble small

Bird receives the 1979 Associated Press Player of the Year Award.

town. Bird's father was an alcoholic. It put a strain on the family. His parents ultimately divorced. Later, Bird's dad took his own life. Basketball allowed Bird to get away from his troubles. He would shoot baskets by himself for hours. He would even practice in the rain and before school. Jim Jones coached Bird at Springs Valley High School.

"He had a great work ethic, always working on [the] fundamentals of the game," Jones said. "Larry just understood how the game should be played."

In high school, Bird developed a following. The "Hick from French Lick" was wowing the local townspeople. He averaged 31 points and 23 rebounds per game during his senior year. Big crowds came to watch the country boy. Bird's final home game attracted thousands.

"His junior year, he was the best player on a very good team," Jones said. "During his senior [year], he became a great player. However, no one envisioned he would become one of the greatest players of all time."

Johnson showed great promise, as well. But he didn't star for his local high school team. Michigan used a special busing system at the time. Some students were bused to schools outside of their

MAGICAL NICKNAME

Family, friends, and teammates had many nicknames for the young Earvin Johnson. They called him "June Bug," "Junior," "E," "Big E," and "Big Fella." Then a sportswriter for the *Lansing State Journal* changed all that. Fred Stabley Jr. attended an Everett High School game in Lansing, Michigan. He watched the 15-year-old Earvin score 36 points, grab 16 rebounds, and record 16 assists. It was a magical performance. Stabley Jr. coined the nickname "Magic." Decades later, Magic is still a household name.

Johnson practices ahead of the 1979 NCAA Final Four.

neighborhoods. The goal was to help integration. For years, much of the United States had been segregated. All-black Sexton High School was only five blocks from Johnson's house. But he was bused several miles away to the all-white Everett High School.

Johnson had never shared the floor with white teammates. The transition was hard at times. The white and black kids at Everett often didn't get along. But basketball helped ease the racial tensions for Johnson. And he proved to be quite the player himself. Johnson was named to Michigan's all-state team in 1975, 1976, and 1977. As a senior, he led Everett to the state title. Johnson scored 34 points in the championship game. It was a sign of things to come.

Indiana University coach Bobby Knight was known both for winning and for having a temper.

CHAPTER 3

Heading to College

Larry Bird earned a basketball scholarship to Indiana University. He was supposed to play for legendary coach Bobby Knight. Bird arrived on campus in the fall of 1974. But he was out of his element in Bloomington, Indiana. He was a small-town, 17-year-old boy. He was a small fish in a sea of 33,000 students. He was overwhelmed and homesick.

Early in the school year, he ran into Knight on campus. Bird said hello. But the gruff basketball coach just kept walking. Bird left school after less than a month. Basketball practice hadn't even started. Bird enrolled in a junior college for a short time. He then took a job for French Lick's Street Department. He cut grass and drove a garbage truck.

IN THE News

Bird didn't feel comfortable at Indiana University. In 1975, he arrived at Indiana State. He quickly became a force to be reckoned with. The *Anderson Herald Bulletin* of Indiana reported on the frenzy surrounding Bird in late 1976.

> Bird-watching, they say, is the rage in Terre Haute these days.... What Bird has done for Indiana State is this: A) pushed the Sycamores to six wins in seven starts; B) given them a player who might make the NCAA's scoring leaders list to be released this week (27.7 points per game) and C) allowed them the great notion they can play with any major college team. Oh, what a feeling. "I think we can play with any team in the nation right now," says Bird. Listen when Larry Bird speaks. His dialogue is slightly above a whisper. He is not inclined to overstate his abilities.

Source: Rick Bozich. "Watching Bird's the ISU Rage." Anderson Herald Bulletin, December 13, 1976. Print. n.p.

In 1975, Bird began classes at Indiana State University in Terre Haute. The school was much smaller than Indiana. When Bird arrived, the basketball team didn't even play in a conference. The Sycamores had never even played in the NCAA Tournament. But Bird felt more at home there.

Bird felt more at home playing at Indiana State.

NCAA rules forced Bird to sit out the 1975–76 season because he transferred. The 6-foot-9, 215-pound forward finally played his first college game the next season. And he was a star. Bird scored in bunches for the Sycamores. Fans were also drawn to his effortless

CHOOSING MICHIGAN STATE

Johnson attended Michigan State games as a high school senior. He would come with his friend Jay Vincent. Johnson was wowed by Spartans star Greg Kelser. In one game, Kelser dunked hard on a 7-foot-5-inch defender. "We got to come here," Johnson said to Vincent. "I want to play with that guy." Johnson and Vincent indeed joined Kelser at Michigan State. They formed a strong trio.

passes. Bird once said, "My feeling about passing is that it don't matter who's doing the scoring as long as it's us."

Indiana State had joined the Missouri Valley Conference (MVC) before the 1976–77 season. It was still a small school from a small-time conference. But the team had Bird. He led the team to a 25–3 record. That was a huge improvement over the 13–12 record one year earlier. Meanwhile, Bird averaged 32.8 points and 13.3 rebounds per game. The team didn't make the NCAA Tournament. It did make the NIT, though.

Meanwhile, a recruiting battle was heating up a few hundred miles north in Michigan. Magic Johnson was a high school senior in 1976–77. Dick Vitale paid an early-morning visit to Johnson's house that winter. Vitale is a famous basketball announcer now. At the time, he was the coach at the University of Detroit. He wanted Johnson to play ball for him. Vitale and his assistant coaches thought they'd catch Johnson at home before leaving for school.

Johnson decided to stay closer to home and play basketball at Michigan State.

But Johnson wasn't there. The 17-year-old was doing what he normally did. He was outside practicing basketball, even though it was cold and snowing.

Colleges across the country wanted Johnson. He got interest from the biggest and best programs. But in the end, it came down to two. Johnson considered the University of Michigan and Michigan State University. Just like Bird, he wanted to stay close to home. Ultimately, he decided to stay in his hometown and attend Michigan State.

Fans around the country heard of Larry Bird, but few had seen him play.

CHAPTER 4

Building the Excitement

Most people learned of Larry Bird in 1977. Magic Johnson was one of them. That November, Bird was on the cover of *Sports Illustrated*. Johnson was impressed by Bird's stats. He was curious about this guy. But he wasn't convinced. Like most people, Johnson didn't know much about Bird.

Johnson and Bird first met in the spring of 1978. Both players were chosen for a team of US college all-stars. The squad competed at the World Invitational Tournament. That's where Johnson got his first taste of Bird's abilities.

The Americans faced the Soviets on April 9. Bird, then 21, grabbed a rebound. The 18-year-old Johnson had already started down the right side of the court. Johnson was calling for the ball. But Bird wasn't delivering. Then it came.

The ball disappeared behind Bird's back. Suddenly the no-look pass ended up in Johnson's right hand. Johnson juked out his defender. The play ended with a Johnson layup. The crowd at Rupp Arena on the University of Kentucky campus erupted. Johnson was convinced.

"This is the baddest white dude I've ever seen in my life," Johnson would say about Bird. "This guy's got game."

Bird was equally impressed with Johnson. He told his brother, "I've just seen the best player in college basketball." From there, the two started to form a respect for each other. They yearned to equal each other's stats.

Both were coming off strong seasons in 1977–78. Bird had been a junior that season. His stats had slipped a bit. But he still put up 30.0 points and 11.5 rebounds per game. Indiana State went 23–9. The team was ranked as high as fourth in the nation at

Bird takes a jump shot in a game against West Texas University in 1978.

DIFFERENT STYLES

Bird and Johnson were both stars on the court. Off the court, the two players had opposite personalities. Johnson was approachable. He was likable. He always seemed to be smiling. But Bird was shy and quiet. He didn't interact with the crowd. He didn't talk to the media much either. He didn't know quite how to deal with that part of his career. He appeared on the cover of *Sports Illustrated* in 1977. But there was no story. He wouldn't agree to an interview. And he didn't like all the attention he got after doing the cover.

one point. However, it once again went to the NIT rather than the NCAA Tournament.

Michigan State had been more successful. Johnson started right away as a freshman. He averaged 17 points, 7.9 rebounds, and 7.4 assists per game. The Spartans went 25–5 and won the Big Ten championship. It was the first time the school had won more than 20 games. Then Michigan State reached the NCAA Tournament's Elite Eight. However, the Spartans lost to eventual champion the University of Kentucky there.

Bird and Johnson had developed followings by then. "Larry Bird Ball" was all the rage in Terre Haute. Bird had his own list of nicknames. The most famous was the "Hick from French Lick." The local TV stations would air Bird basketball highlights. Indiana State

Magic Johnson had wowed fans by leading Michigan State to a Big Ten Conference championship as a freshman in 1978.

Johnson dribbles against a University of Kentucky player during the 1978 NCAA Tournament.

students would skip class to stand in line for game tickets. Sales for season tickets tripled.

Bird was recognized nationally as a first-team All-American. The Boston Celtics noticed Bird, too. They made him the sixth overall pick in the NBA Draft. But outside of the MVC, few people had seen Bird play. Small college basketball games weren't shown on national TV in those days. Even Bird felt he had more to do in college. Though the Celtics kept his rights, Bird returned to Indiana State for his senior season.

Johnson was better known. Playing at a bigger school, he had shown great promise and flair. Fans were drawn to his exciting

IN THE News

Larry Bird developed a reputation at Indiana State. A January 1978 Sports Illustrated article talked about the buzz he was creating back home in French Lick:

> It is no wonder that Bird, a junior forward at Indiana State, and his points per game are the subjects of constant concern among the 2,059 folks in French Lick. He is the town's celebrity, having gone in the last couple of years from driving a garbage truck and hunting mushrooms thereabouts to playing basketball in Bulgaria and getting his picture on magazine covers in Italy, not to mention the U. S. of A. Bird was the top scorer for a while this season, but his average has dropped a bit lately, and folks are naturally wondering if something is wrong. Maybe he should practice shooting a rubber ball through a bottomless coffee can again, the way he did as a kid.

Source: Larry Keith. "Bird Has Those Trees at the Top." Sports Illustrated. Time Inc., January 23, 1978. Web. Accessed June 25, 2014.

playing style. They never knew when he was going to make a no-look pass or set up an alley-oop. Yet even so, Johnson was a third-team All-American as a freshman. Both Johnson and Bird were reserves for the US team at the World Invitational Tournament. It would not be long, however, before both were national superstars.

Bird looks for space during a 1979 game against New Mexico State University.

CHAPTER 5

Game Time

Indiana State and Michigan State were both considered good basketball teams going into the 1978–79 season. But neither team was great. And neither was expected to change the future of college basketball.

Now a sophomore, Magic Johnson became a special player. He averaged 16.1 points, 8.2 assists, and 7.4 rebounds per game. But it was his flashy playing style that won over fans. Johnson could play all over the court. His passing and big-play ability stood out. Meanwhile, Greg Kelser was the Spartans' leading scorer. The future NBA first-round draft pick averaged 18.1 points per game. Together, the duo led Michigan State to a 22–6 record. They also won another Big Ten title.

Larry Bird had already proven to be a special player. Again, though, few had an opportunity to see him. The Sycamores

LARRY BIRD IS WHITE?

The Internet didn't exist in March 1979. ESPN wouldn't launch for another six months. Indiana State was hardly on national television before the NCAA Tournament. The general public didn't know much about Larry Bird and his team. And even some of the Michigan State players thought he was black. "We thought Larry Bird was a black guy in Indiana, killing everybody. He's scoring 35 a game? He's gotta be a brother!" Michigan State's Greg Kelser would jokingly recall years later.

played just three games on national TV during his senior season. Bird averaged 28.6 points and 14.9 rebounds per game. His legend grew as he led the team to an undefeated regular season. The Sycamores came into the postseason ranked number one in the nation. Bird was on his way to winning the major national player of the year awards. He would also end his career as the fifth-highest scorer in NCAA history.

The NCAA Tournament expanded from 32 to 40 teams in 1979. At-large entries joined the conference champions. And that year, teams were seeded for the first time. Indiana State earned one of the four number-one seeds. Michigan State was a two seed.

Bird makes his way through a crowd of fans after leading Indiana State to a 73–71 win over Arkansas in the 1979 Elite Eight.

Both teams had a bye in the first round. So they each had to win three games to reach the Final Four. Michigan State won those games easily. Indiana State had more trouble. Bird had suffered a broken thumb during the MVC tournament. The University of Arkansas nearly upset the Sycamores in the Elite Eight. But Bird and his teammates squeezed out a 63–61 win. They were on to the Final Four.

Bird defends against a DePaul player during the 1979 Final Four.

There was a buzz ahead of the Final Four. Fans had followed Bird and Johnson throughout the season. They were eager to see the two stars face off in Salt Lake City. First, though, the teams had to win their semifinals.

Indiana State played DePaul University. DePaul was the second seed in the West Region. Bird hardly played like a man with a broken thumb. He had 35 points, 16 rebounds, and nine assists. Still, the Sycamores only squeaked by with a two-point win. Michigan

IN THE News

Johnson was known for his charisma. Bird was much quieter and reserved. This was particularly true when he was around the media. That trend continued at the 1979 Final Four.

> Throughout the season, Larry Bird had fulfilled his virtual vow of silence. He had talked on TV a few times, he had traveled to New York last week to receive an award. "And when you receive an award," Bill Hodges had told him "you talk." And after Saturday's game, he had answered a few questions about it. But mostly, he had been the Silent Sycamore, a country bumpkin apparently who didn't know what to say.
>
> Source: Dave Anderson. "Herb Shriner with a Jumper." New York Times, March 26, 1979. Print. C6.

State had an easier time. It played the University of Pennsylvania. Penn was an underdog as a nine seed. It showed. Johnson recorded a triple-double. The Spartans rolled to a 101–67 win.

Finally, it was time. On one side was the charismatic showman nicknamed Magic. On the other was Bird, the "Hick from French Lick," with a deadly shot and workmanlike style. They would finally play on March 26.

One day earlier, the teams went through a final practice. Johnson got to role-play again. This time, he got to be Bird. It was exciting for Johnson. He told a reporter, "I got to pretend I was Larry Bird." The Sycamores took the court right after the Spartans. Just to rattle them, the Sycamore players showed up early and wore cowboy hats. Johnson and his teammates didn't know what to make of Bird and these country boys. But they weren't rattled.

The Final Four took place at the University of Utah's Special Events Center. The official attendance for the final was 15,410. Approximately 35 million tuned into the final game on TV. The Spartans were ready. They started the game fast and never looked back.

Bird came into the game averaging 30.3 points with 13.3 rebounds per game. But he was double- and triple-teamed by Michigan State defenders. They held him to only 19 points. Bird's frustration was showing toward the end of the game. He knocked the ball out of Johnson's hand while he was inbounding. It was an automatic technical foul. Later, as was becoming routine in

Johnson dunks the ball against Indiana State during the 1979 NCAA championship game.

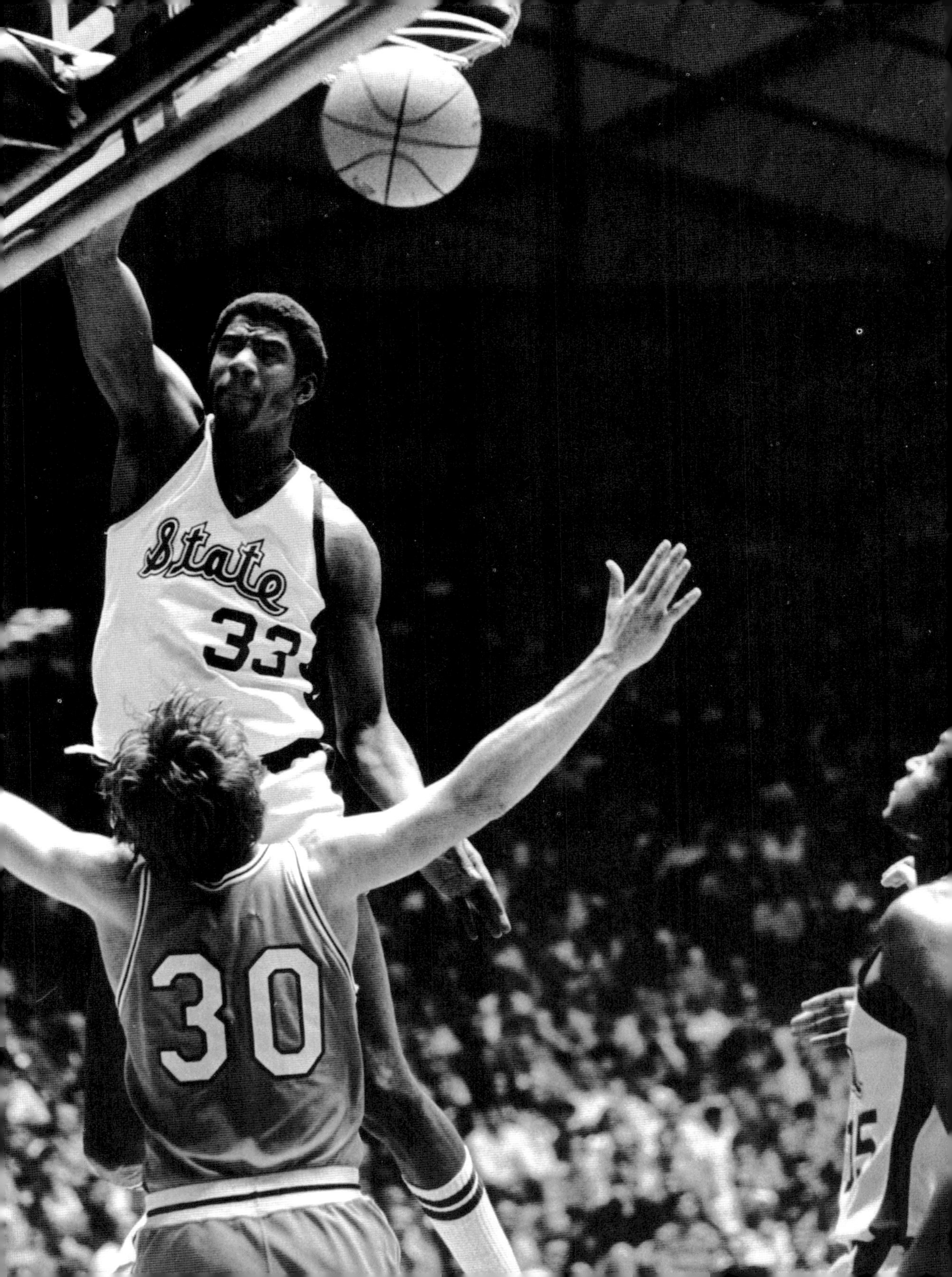
State
33
30

this game, Johnson lobbed a pass to Kelser. Up by 10 points with only 10 seconds left in the game, Kelser dunked the ball. It put an exclamation point on the game. With a 75–64 win, the Spartans handed the Sycamores their first loss.

Johnson scored 24 points and had seven rebounds in the championship game. He was named Most Outstanding Player of the Final Four. After the game, Johnson and his teammates celebrated. Bird sat on the bench with his face buried in a white towel.

The game proved to be not as exciting as fans hoped. But it was a turning point for college basketball. What is now known as March Madness and the rivalry between Johnson and Bird was born. The final still ranks as the highest-rated game in the history of televised basketball.

Johnson cuts down the net as NCAA champion after his Michigan State Spartans beat Bird's Indiana State Sycamores in the 1979 championship game.

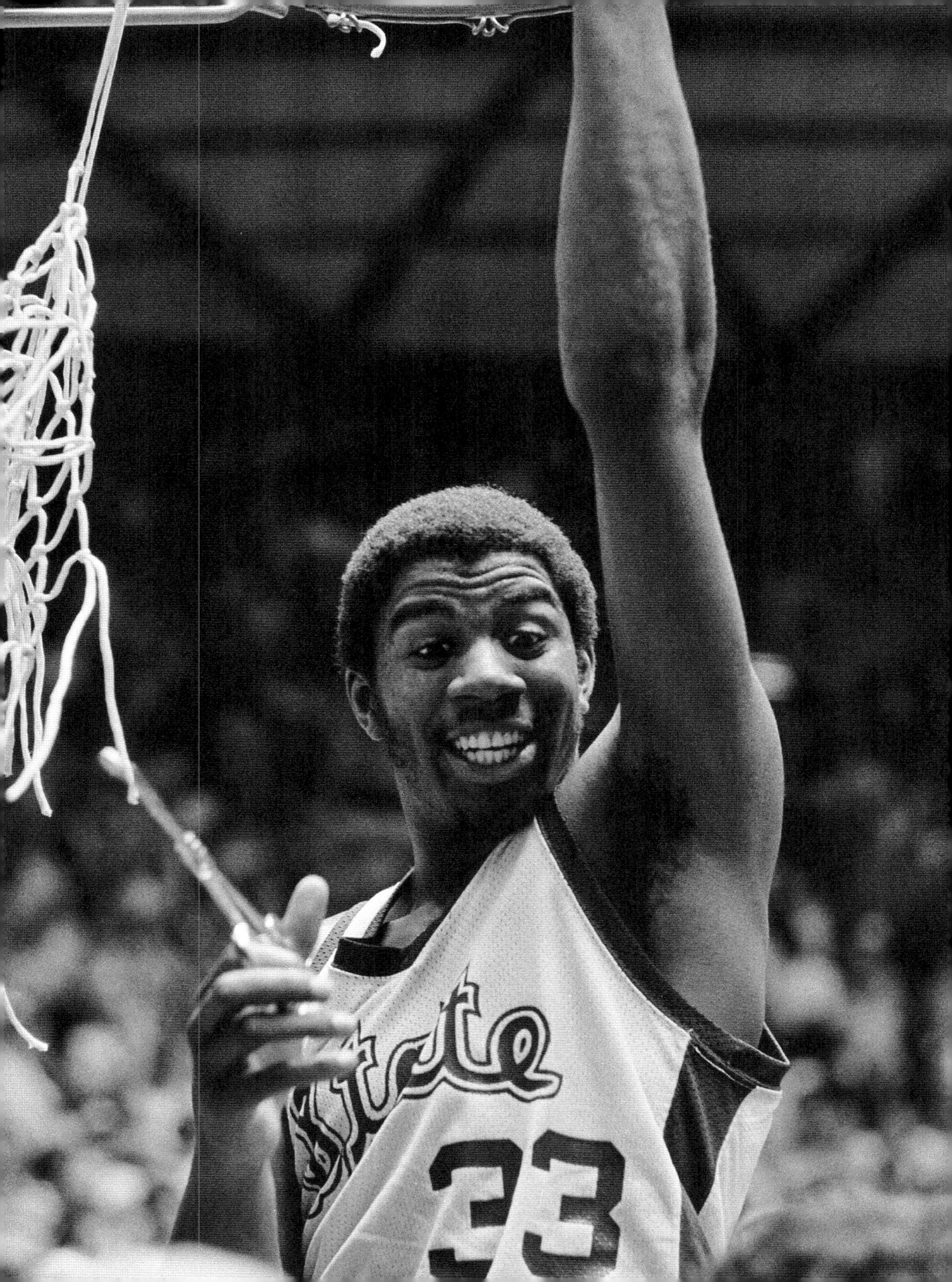
33

KENTUCKY
30
UCONN
2
THE ROAD ENDS HERE
UCONN
11
KENTUCKY
5
UCONN
13
FGM
21/49

Nearly 80,000 fans pack AT&T Stadium to watch the 2014 NCAA championship game.

CHAPTER 6

Legacy

A crowd of 79,238 fans filled AT&T Stadium in north Texas. Former presidents George W. Bush and Bill Clinton watched from luxury boxes. They weren't there to watch the Dallas Cowboys, though. This was the 2014 NCAA championship game. The Final Four had come a long way since 1979.

Today's NCAA Tournament is a month-long event. Fans call it March Madness. Sixty-eight teams begin the tournament. Some are big-school teams with famous players. Other teams come from small conferences. Upsets are common. Fans love the matchups and the drama. Some even take time off from work to watch. All around the country, people fill out brackets. They try to guess which teams will advance.

IN THE News

The 1979 NCAA championship game took place on March 26. Thirty years later, *Washington Post* columnist Michael Wilbon reflected on that game's impact.

> Magic Johnson and Larry Bird did this. With all due respect to John Wooden and his 10 championships at UCLA, the Bruins dominated what was then merely a basketball tournament. But Magic and Bird, 30 years ago Thursday night, gave us March Madness. Now, what we know in retrospect is that it was one of the most groundbreaking sporting events in America the last 40 years, one that launched the popularity of college basketball and began the Golden Age of professional basketball. And without that game, March might be just another month.

Source: Michael Wilbon. "Bird vs. Magic 1979 NCAA Championship Game Launched March Madness." *Washington Post.* The Washington Post Co., March 26, 2009. Web. Accessed June 25, 2014.

This hysteria all began in 1979. Interest in college basketball steadily grew into the 1980s. ESPN played a major role in that. The 24-hour sports channel debuted in September 1979. The network provided more coverage of college basketball than had ever been available. TV helped bring the drama of the win-or-go-home tournament to life.

Between 1970 and 1979, the average attendance for the championship game was 17,916. It grew to 31,248 during the 1980s. The Final Four began to outgrow basketball arenas during the 1980s. All of the Final Fours since 1997 have been held in large domed stadiums. From 2010 to 2012, the average championship game attendance was 70,740.

TV viewership skyrocketed as well. That led major TV networks to bid aggressively for the rights to show the tournament. CBS paid $7,500 to be able to broadcast the 1940 championship game. In 1973, TV rights exceeded $1 million for the first time. CBS and Turner Sports bought the rights in 2010. They agreed to pay close to $11 billion to show the next 14 tournaments.

Magic Johnson and Larry Bird impacted the professional game as well. Bird signed with the Boston Celtics after the NCAA title game. His contract paid him $3.25 million in five years. It made him the highest-paid rookie in the history of team sports at that time. Johnson also joined the NBA that year. The Los Angeles Lakers selected him first overall in that 1979 draft.

The NBA suffered from a variety of problems at the time. Fans were losing interest. TV ratings were low. A league-wide drug problem also hurt the NBA's image. Bird and Johnson took the lead in rebuilding it. The Celtics and Lakers became contenders right away in 1979–80. The stardom Bird and Johnson earned in college followed them to the NBA. The flashy Johnson led the "Showtime" Lakers. His up-tempo style made the Lakers one of the league's most exciting teams. Celtics fans, meanwhile, embraced Bird's blue-collar work ethic. Bird was rarely the most athletic player on the court. But he became a great defender. Plus, he was one of the NBA's all-time best shooters. In 1984, their teams met in the NBA Finals. It was the most-watched basketball championship series of its time. Bird and the Celtics won that round. But Johnson and Los Angeles came back to beat Boston in the 1985 and 1987 NBA Finals.

BECOMING FRIENDS

Johnson and Bird's rivalry began during their college days. However, it grew even stronger during their NBA days. During the mid-1980s, Converse hired Johnson and Bird to pitch their basketball shoes. The two stars agreed to do a commercial together. But the commercial was filmed in Bird's hometown of French Lick, Indiana. Johnson wasn't thrilled about the location. But Bird's mom greeted Johnson with a hug. The Lakers star also ate lunch at his house. He was sold after that. Johnson and Bird got to know each other during that time and became lasting friends.

Bird and Johnson, shown at the 2009 Final Four, later became friends.

From 1980 to 1991, Los Angeles reached the Finals nine times and won five. Boston played in five NBA Finals and won three. By the time they passed the torch to Michael Jordan in the 1990s, the NBA was as popular and profitable as ever. And thanks to the excitement surrounding their 1979 NCAA Tournament, March is now always filled with madness.

TIMELINE

December 7, 1956
Larry Joe Bird is born in West Baden, Indiana.

1974
Bird, a 6-foot-9-inch senior, averages 30.6 points, 20.6 rebounds, and 4.3 assists for Springs Valley High School.

1976
In Bird's first game with Indiana State, he has a triple-double—31 points, 18 rebounds, 10 assists—in an 81–60 win over Chicago State University.

1978
Drafted sixth overall as a junior by the Boston Celtics, Bird decides to return to Indiana State for his senior year.

March 26, 1979
In a much anticipated NCAA championship game, Johnson and the the Spartans beat Bird and previously undefeated Sycamores 75–64 in Salt Lake City.

March 27, 1939
Oregon defeats Ohio State 46–33 to win the first NCAA basketball tournament.

August 14, 1959
Earvin Johnson Jr. is born in Lansing, Michigan.

1974
Lansing State Journal sportswriter Fred Stabley Jr. gives Johnson the nickname "Magic" after he scores 36 points and gets 18 rebounds and 16 assists in an Everett High School game.

1978
As a freshman, Johnson leads Michigan State to a 25–5 record and its first Big Ten Conference title in 19 seasons.

1979
Bird leads Indiana State to the NCAA final with a 33–0 record. Johnson leads Michigan State to the championship game with a 26–6 record.

1979
Bird signs a five-year, $3.25 million deal, the largest rookie contract in sports history, with the Celtics. Johnson is the number one pick by the Los Angeles Lakers in the NBA draft.

GLOSSARY

All-American
A college athlete chosen as one of the best in his or her sport for a given season.

at-large
Bids to the NCAA Tournament given to teams that did not win their conference.

blue collar
Working class.

busing
The practice of transporting students to schools in different communities in an effort to integrate black and white students.

integrated
When people of different races were brought together after being legally separated.

peer
One that equals another.

recruiting
The process of a college or university trying to attract a student-athlete to play a sport or sports at its school.

rival
Person or team that brings out intense emotions in an opponent and its fans.

scholarship
Money given to a student to help pay for further education.

seeding
When a competitor or team is given a ranking for the purposes of the draw in a tournament. The NCAA Tournament has four regions, each with teams seeded one through 16.

segregated
Separated or divided based on some characteristic, such as sex or race.

triple-double
When a basketball player records double-digits (at least 10) in three different stat categories in one game.

FOR MORE INFORMATION

SELECTED BIBLIOGRAPHY

Bird, Larry, and Earvin Johnson. *When the Game Was Ours*. Boston: Houghton Mifflin Harcourt, 2009. Print.

Moran, Malcolm. "Johnson: Magical by Nature: Quick, Startling Passes Loves to Talk." *New York Times*, March 25, 1979. Print. Sports: C6.

Moran, Malcolm. "Spartans Used No Cues to Silence Larry Bird: Magic as Imitator Memo from Bird." *New York Times*, March 27, 1979. Print. Sports: C15.

Rohan, Jack. "N.C.A.A. Final Preview: Jack Rohan's Scouting Report." *New York Times*, March 27, 1979. Print. Sports: C1, C6.

UPI. "Earvin to play for Spartans." *Traverse City Record-Eagle*, April 22, 1977. Print. 13.

FURTHER READINGS

Davis, Seth. *When March Went Mad: The Game that Transformed Basketball*. New York: Times Books, 2009. Print.

Frei, Terry. *March 1939: Before the Madness: The Story of the First NCAA Basketball Tournament Champions*. Lanham, MD: Taylor Trade Publishing, 2014. Print.

Hager, Tom. *The Ultimate Book of March Madness: The Players, Games, and Cinderellas that Captivated a Nation*. Minneapolis, MN: MVP Books, 2012. Print.

Roselius, J Chris. *Magic Johnson: Basketball Star & Entrepreneur*. Edina, MN: Abdo Publishing Co., 2011. Print.

WEBSITES

To learn more about the Greatest Events in Sports History, visit **booklinks.abdopublishing.com**. These links are routinely monitored and updated to provide the most current information available.

PLACES TO VISIT

The College Basketball Experience
1401 Grand Boulevard
Kansas City, MO 64106
(816) 949-7500
www.collegebasketballexperience.com
This is an interactive entertainment facility connected to the Sprint Center, which has hosted NCAA men's and women's basketball tournaments. It houses the National Collegiate Basketball Hall of Fame, where visitors can learn about the history of the game.

Naismith Memorial Basketball Hall of Fame
1000 Hall of Fame Avenue
Springfield, MA 01105
(877) 446-6752
www.hoophall.com
The Naismith Memorial Basketball Hall of Fame is home to more than 300 inductees and a vast amount of basketball history. The museum, located on the banks of the Connecticut River, is named for Dr. Naismith, who invented the sport more than a century ago.

INDEX

Big Ten Conference, 24, 29
Bing, Dave, 9
Bird, Larry
  childhood, 9–12
  college, 5, 15–18, 21–22, 24, 26–27, 29–34, 36, 40
  friendship with Johnson, 42
  high school, 11–12
  NBA, 41–42
Boston Celtics, 26, 41, 42–43
Bush, George W., 39
Chamberlain, Wilt, 9
Clinton, Bill, 39
DePaul University, 32
Detroit Pistons, 9
Indiana State University, 16, 18, 22, 24, 26, 27, 29, 30–32
Johnson, Earvin "Magic"
  childhood, 9
  college, 5, 21–22, 24, 26–27, 29, 32, 33, 34, 36, 40
  friendship with Bird, 42
  high school, 12–13, 18–19
  NBA, 41–42
  nickname, 12
Jordan, Michael, 43

Kelser, Greg, 18, 29, 30, 36
Knight, Bobby, 15
Los Angeles Lakers, 41–42
March Madness, 5, 6, 7, 36, 39, 40
Michigan State University, 18, 19, 24, 29, 30–31, 32–33, 34
Missouri Valley Conference, 18
National Basketball Association (NBA), 9, 10, 26, 29, 41, 42–43
National Collegiate Athletic Association (NCAA), 5, 6, 7, 16, 17, 40, 41
National Invitation Tournament (NIT), 7, 18, 24
NCAA Tournament, 16, 18, 24
  1979, 30–36, 39, 40, 43
  2014, 39
  expansion, 7, 30, 39
  Final Four, 6, 30–32, 33, 34, 36, 39, 41
  history, 5–7
  TV, 5, 30, 40–41
Northwestern University, 5
Ohio State University, 6

Philadelphia 76ers, 9
Sports Illustrated, 21, 24, 27
University of Detroit, 18
University of Oregon, 6–7
University of Pennsylvania, 33
Vitale, Dick, 18
World Invitational Tournament, 21, 27

ABOUT THE AUTOR

P. K. Daniel is an editor, reporter, and writer. This is her second book. She spent 15 years at the *San Diego Union-Tribune*, where she was recognized with a Special Merit award for editing, a U-Team award for collaboration, and several headline-writing honors. Her work has appeared in *Baseball America*, *SB Nation Longform*, TeamUSA.org, *U-T San Diego*, the *Washington Post*, *Lower Extremity Review*, and *Sport Magazine*.